A Christmas Star

and other Christmas Stories

Miles Kelly

First published in 2015 by Miles Kelly Publishing Ltd
Harding's Barn, Bardfield End Green, Thaxted, Essex, CM6 3PX, UK

2 4 6 8 10 9 7 5 3 1

Publishing Director Belinda Gallagher
Creative Director Jo Cowan
Editorial Director Rosie Neave
Senior Editor Sarah Parkin
Design Manager Joe Jones
Production Elizabeth Collins, Caroline Kelly
Reprographics Stephan Davis, Jennifer Cozens, Thom Allaway

ISBN 978-1-78209-825-6

Printed in China

British Library Cataloguing-in-Publication Data
A catalogue record for this book is available from the British Library

ACKNOWLEDGEMENTS
The publishers would like to thank the following artists who have contributed to this book:

Front cover: Simona Sanfilippo (Plum Pudding Illustration Agency)

Inside illustrations:
Decorative frame Rachel Cloyne (Pickled Ink)
Cutting the Christmas Tree Charlotte Cooke (The Bright Agency)
Matthew Insists on Puffed Sleeves Florencia Denis (Plum Pudding Illustration Agency)
A Christmas Star Antonia Woodward (Plum Pudding Illustration Agency)
Little Roger's Night in the Church Natalia Moore (Advocate Art)

Made with paper from a sustainable forest

www.mileskelly.net
info@mileskelly.net

Contents

Cutting the Christmas Tree

An extract from *Peter and Polly in Winter*
by Rose Lucia

*Traditionally, in America, Christmas trees
were decorated with strings of popcorn.*

*I*t was nearly Christmas. Peter could not wait for the day to come. He kept saying, "Mother, will it be Christmas tomorrow?"

At last Father said, "Do you want Christmas before I get the tree?"

"No," said Peter. "But will you ever get the tree?"

"I will today. You and Polly may go with me. We will choose the prettiest fir tree we can find. Put on your things, and we will start now."

"Oh, goody, goody!" cried Peter, jumping up and down. "Now I know that Christmas is almost here."

"It will be here tomorrow," said Father. "Run and tell Polly."

They went through the field at the back of the house. They climbed over the stone-wall post office.

"We must find a strong tree, my boy. Can you see one you like?"

"That one," said Peter.

Father laughed. "That is a strong tree. But it is too tall. We should have to cut a hole in the ceiling to stand it up. Find a smaller one."

"There is a good tree. See how pretty it is. It looks like our little firs at home."

"I believe that is just right for us, Polly. I will cut it down. Please hold my coat."

Father swung his axe. He gave three sharp blows. But all at once there was a chatter overhead.

In the next tree a grey squirrel was running up a large branch. He was scolding with all his might. His tail was jerking. He looked very cross.

"Well, old fellow," said Father, "did I disturb you? I am sorry. Go back to sleep. We will not take your tree."

"His is too bare, isn't it, Father? The leaves have all gone. We must have a fir tree for ours. It has queer leaves. But they do not fall off in the winter."

"That is why we call such trees evergreens, Polly. They are always green. Pine trees are evergreens, too. Their needles are longer than fir needles."

Soon father had cut down the fir. He put it over his shoulder, and the end dragged on the snow.

"Now we are ready for home," he said. "Tonight Mother and I will dress this tree. Tomorrow you may see it."

"Have you really a dress for it?" asked Peter. "I hope it is red. Who made it?"

"Oh Peter, how silly you are! Father means dress it up with candy bags and popped corn and presents."

"I know now," said Peter. "Ponies and guns and things."

"See the snow sparkle, children. The sun makes it do that. Look at the blue sky. Doesn't the air feel good to you?"

"It makes me feel like running," said Polly, excitedly.

"Then run along, chicks. You will get home first. Tell Mother that the Christmas tree is really coming. You may pop the corn this afternoon."

When Peter and Polly got home, they ran into the house.

"Mother, Mother!" they shouted. "The Christmas tree is coming. Father has it."

"Why, Mother," said Polly, "what makes the house smell so sweet? For it smells just like the woods."

"It is the green wreaths, Polly. I have them in all the rooms. There is one on the front door, too. These wreaths smell better

than the ones that we buy. You may help me make the rest of them. We need more."

So the children went into the kitchen. On a table were pieces of evergreen boughs. They helped their mother twist the pieces into circles. On each circle she wound many small twigs. When done, the wreaths were firm and thick and green.

"How good it does smell, Mother. I like Christmas smells. But see my hands."

"That is the pitch from the greens, Polly. Just rub on a little butter. It will take off the pitch. Then wash your hands in warm water. I will clean up the rest of the greens. When this is done, we will pop our corn."

That was always fun. Polly liked to shake the popper. She liked to see the white kernels of corn hop up and down. She liked the good smell, too.

Soon two large panfuls were popped. Then came another task. The corn must be strung. Polly and Peter both helped. But, of course, mother could string much faster than they. She told them stories while they worked.

"Now, children, the Giveaway Box is ready. You may choose your things to give away."

On the floor in the dining room there was a large box. It was filled with games, dolls, bags of candy and popped corn, and many other things.

These were for Peter and Polly to give away. They would make other children happy. And that would make Peter and Polly happy, too.

Peter chose a jumping jack for Tim.
Polly chose to give him a whistle.
When Polly was out of the room,
Peter chose a present for her. It was
the prettiest doll he had ever seen.
Polly chose a train of cars to
give to Peter.

"I think Mrs White
would like this
candlestick," said Polly.
Then Mother said,
"Why don't you give the hot water bag to
Grandmother? Her bag leaks."

"Oh, we will!" cried both children.

"There is my teacher," said Peter. "I will
give her these marbles."

"Your teacher! You don't go to school,
Peter," Polly said.

"I did one day," said Peter. "I like her. She

was good to me. She is my teacher. I don't care what you say."

"Never mind about that, chicks," said Mother. "I'm afraid she hasn't a pocket for the marbles. Why don't you give her the box of handkerchiefs?"

Before long the Giveaway Box was empty. Every friend in the village had been remembered. Peter and Polly were tired. They were glad when it was bedtime.

As Mother tucked her up, Polly said, "I like the Giveaway Box. It is fun. It is as much fun as it is to get things. You gave it to us, Mother. You give us everything."

"Father, too," said Mother. "It makes fathers and mothers happy to do that."

Matthew Insists on Puffed Sleeves

An extract from *Anne of Green Gables*
by L M Montgomery

Anne Shirley has been adopted by Marilla and her brother Matthew. She has always longed for fashionable puffed sleeves, but Marilla makes her dresses with plain sleeves.

*M*atthew was having a bad ten minutes of it. He had come into the kitchen, in the twilight of a cold, grey December evening, and had sat down in the woodbox corner to take off his heavy boots, unconscious of the fact that Anne

and a bevy of her schoolmates were having a practice in the sitting room. Presently the girls came trooping through the hall and out into the kitchen, laughing and chattering gaily. They did not see Matthew, who watched them shyly for ten minutes as they put on caps and jackets and talked about the concert.

Anne stood among them, as bright-eyed as they, but Matthew suddenly became conscious that there was something about her that was different from her mates. Anne had a brighter face, and bigger, starrier eyes, and more delicate features than the others. The difference that disturbed him did not consist in any of these respects. Then in what did it consist?

Eventually Matthew arrived at a solution to his problem. Anne was not dressed like the other girls!

The more Matthew thought about the matter the more he was convinced that Anne never had been dressed like the other girls – never since she had come to Green Gables. Marilla kept her clothed in plain, dark dresses, all made after the same unvarying pattern. He was quite sure that Anne's sleeves did not look like the sleeves that the other girls wore. He recalled the cluster of girls he had seen around her that evening and wondered why Marilla always kept Anne so plainly and soberly gowned.

Of course, it must be all right. Marilla knew best and Marilla was bringing her up. But surely it would do no harm to let the child have one pretty dress. Matthew decided that he would give her one. Christmas was only a fortnight off. A nice new dress would be the very thing for a present. Matthew, with a sigh of satisfaction, put away his pipe and went to bed, while Marilla opened all the doors and aired the house.

When Matthew came to think the matter over he decided that a woman was required to cope with the situation. Marilla was out of the question. Matthew felt sure she would throw cold water on his project at once. There remained only Mrs Lynde, for of no other woman in Avonlea would Matthew have dared to ask advice. To

Mrs Lynde he went accordingly, and that good lady promptly took the matter out of the harassed man's hands.

"Pick out a dress for you to give Anne? To be sure I will. I'm going to Carmody tomorrow and I'll attend to it. Have you something particular in mind? No? Well, I'll just go by my own judgment then. I believe a nice rich brown would just suit Anne. Perhaps you'd like me to make it up for her, too, seeing that if Marilla was to make it Anne would probably get wind of it before the time and spoil the surprise? Well, I'll do it. I'll make it to fit my niece, Jenny Gillis, for she and Anne are as alike as two peas as far as figure goes."

"Well now, I'm much obliged," said Matthew, "and – and – I dunno – but I'd like – I think they make the sleeves

different nowadays to what they used to be. If it wouldn't be asking too much I – I'd like them made in the new way."

"Puffs? Of course. You needn't worry about it, Matthew. I'll make it up in the very latest fashion," Mrs Lynde said to him.

To herself she added when Matthew had gone, "It'll be a real satisfaction to see that poor child wearing something decent for once. The way Marilla dresses her is positively ridiculous, that's what, and I've ached to tell her so plainly a dozen times."

Marilla knew all the following fortnight that Matthew had something on his mind, but what it was she could not guess, until Christmas Eve, when Mrs Lynde brought up the new dress.

"So this is what Matthew has been looking so mysterious over and grinning about to himself for two weeks, is it?" she said a little stiffly, but tolerantly. "I knew he was up to some foolishness. Well, I must say I don't think Anne needed any more dresses. I hope she'll be satisfied at last, for I know she's been hankering after those silly sleeves ever since they came in."

Christmas morning broke on a beautiful white world. It had been very mild, but just enough snow fell softly in the night to transfigure Avonlea. Anne peeped out from her frosted gable window with delighted eyes. The ploughed fields were stretches of snowy dimples, and there was a crisp tang in the air. She ran downstairs singing until her voice re-echoed through Green Gables.

"Merry Christmas, Marilla! Merry Christmas, Matthew! Isn't it a lovely Christmas? I'm so glad it's white. I don't like

green Christmases. They're not green – they're just faded browns and greys. Why – Matthew, is that for me? Oh, Matthew!"

Matthew had unfolded the dress from its paper swathings and held it out to her.

Anne took the dress and looked at it. Oh, how pretty it was – a lovely soft brown with all the gloss of silk, a skirt with dainty frills and a little ruffle of filmy lace at the neck. But the sleeves – they were the crowning glory! Long elbow cuffs, and above them two beautiful puffs divided bows of brown-silk ribbon.

"That's a Christmas present for you, Anne," said Matthew shyly. "Why – why – don't you like it? Well now – well now."

For Anne's eyes had filled with tears.

"Like it! Oh, Matthew!" Anne laid the dress over a chair and clasped her hands.

"Matthew, it's perfectly exquisite. Oh, I can never thank you enough. Look at those sleeves! Oh, this must be a happy dream."

"Well, well, let us have breakfast," interrupted Marilla. "I must say, Anne, I don't think you needed the dress, but since Matthew has got it for you, see that you take good care of it. There's a hair ribbon Mrs Lynde left for you. It's brown, to match the dress. Come now, sit down."

"I don't see how I'm going to eat breakfast," said Anne rapturously. "I'd rather feast my eyes on that dress. It was lovely of Mrs Lynde to give me the ribbon too. I feel that I ought to be a very good girl. I will make an extra effort after this."

A Christmas Star

Adapted from a story
by Katharine Pyle

"Come now, my dear little stars," said Mother Moon. "I will tell you a story." Every morning for a week before Christmas, Mother Moon used to call all the little stars around her and tell them stories about wonderful stars. Then the stars would bid Mother Moon goodnight and go to bed in the sky chamber, for the stars' bedtime is when people are beginning to waken and see that it is morning.

But that particular morning, one golden star still lingered beside Mother Moon.

"What is the matter, my little star?" asked Mother Moon.

"Oh, Mother Moon," said the golden star. "I am so sad! I wish I could shine for someone's heart like that star of wonder that you tell us about."

"Why, aren't you happy up here in the sky country?" asked Mother Moon.

"Yes," said the star, "but tonight it seems as if I must find some heart to shine for."

"Then if that is so," said Mother Moon, "the time has come, my little star, for you to go through the Wonder Hall."

"The Wonder Hall? What is that?" asked the star.

Rising, Mother Moon took the little star by the hand and led it to a door that it had

never seen before. Mother Moon opened the door and there was a long dark hall. At the far end shone a little speck of light.

"What is this?" asked the star.

"It is the Wonder Hall, and it is through this that you must go to find the heart where you belong," said Mother Moon.

So the little star stepped into the Wonder Hall, and the door of the sky house closed behind it.

The next thing the star knew it was hanging in a toy shop with a whole row of other stars, which were blue and red and silver. The little star itself was gold.

The shop smelled of evergreen, and was full of Christmas shoppers, men and women and children.

But the star looked at no one but a little boy standing in front of the counter, for as

soon as the star saw the child it
knew that he was the one
to whom it belonged.
The little boy was
standing beside a sweet-faced
woman and he was not looking at
anything in particular. The star
shook and trembled on the string
that held it, because it was afraid
the child would not see it.

The lady had a number of toys
on the counter before her, and she was
saying, "Now I think we have presents for
everyone. There's the doll for Lou, and the
game for Ned, and the music box for May,
and then the rocking horse and the sled."

Suddenly the little boy caught her by the
arm. "Oh, Mother," he said. He had just
seen the star.

"Well, what is it darling?" asked the lady.

"Oh, Mother, just see that star up there! I wish – oh, I do wish I had it."

"Oh, my dear, we have so many things for the Christmas tree," said the mother.

"Yes, I know, but I do want the star," said the child.

"Very well," said the mother, smiling, "then we will take that, too."

So the star was taken down from where it hung and wrapped up in a piece of paper, and all the while it thrilled with joy, for now it belonged to the little boy.

It was not until the afternoon before Christmas, when the tree was being decorated, that the golden star was unwrapped and taken out from the paper.

"Here is something else," said the sweet-faced lady. "We must hang this on the tree."

"Oh, yes," said someone else who was helping to decorate the tree, "we will hang it here on the very top."

So the little star hung on the highest branch of the Christmas tree.

That evening all the candles were lit on the Christmas tree. The gold and silver balls, the fairies and the glass fruits shone and twinkled in the light, and high above them all shone the golden star.

At seven o'clock the folding doors of the room where the Christmas tree

stood were thrown open, and a crowd of children came trooping in.

They laughed and shouted and all talked together, and after a while there was music, and then presents were taken from the Christmas tree and given to all of them.

The star had never been so happy in all its life, for the little boy was there.

The little boy stood apart from the other children, looking up at the star with his hands clasped behind him.

At last it was all over. The lights were put out, the children went home and the house grew still. Then the ornaments on the Christmas tree began to talk among themselves.

"So that is all over," said a silver ball.

"Yes," said a glass bunch of grapes, "the best of it is over. Of course people will come to look at us for several days yet, but it won't be like this evening."

"And then we'll be laid away for another year," said a paper fairy. "It seems hardly worthwhile. Such a few days out of the year and then to be shut up in the box again."

The bunch of grapes was wrong in saying that people would come to look at the Christmas tree the next few days, for nobody came near it. Everybody in the house went about very quietly, with anxious faces, for the little boy was ill.

At last, one evening, a nurse came into the room and took the golden star. She carried it out into the hall and upstairs to a room where the little boy lay.

The sweet-faced lady was sitting by the bed, and as the nurse came in she held out her hand for the star.

"Is this what you wanted, my darling?" she asked, bending over the little boy.

The child nodded and held out his hands for the star, and as he clasped it a wonderful, shining smile came over his face. Then he fell asleep, holding the star tightly.

"Thank goodness," said the nurse. "I was worried for a while, but I'm sure now that he'll be fit and well again in no time."

And it was so. As long as the boy lived, he put the star on the top of his Christmas tree. And for the rest of the year, the golden star twinkled on a string in the window.

Little Roger's Night in the Church

By Susan Coolidge

*I*t was Christmas Eve. Little Roger sat in his grandparents' house eating his supper. Grandfather had gone to the church to put the fire in order for the night, lock up the doors and make all safe.

Suddenly Granny exclaimed, "Oh deary me! Grandfather has forgotten his keys. Would you be afraid to run up with them?"

"Not a bit," said Roger. "I'll take 'em down in a minute, and then run home."

So, after a goodnight hug from Granny, off he ran. The church was near, and the moon light as day, so he never thought of being afraid. Grandfather was stooping to cover the fire for the night. He never knew Roger was there till he jingled the keys in his ear, but he laughed, well pleased.

"I only just missed them," he said. "You're a good boy to fetch them up. Are you going home with me tonight?"

"No, I'm to sleep at my mother's," said Roger, "but I'll wait and walk with you, Grandfather." So he slipped into a pew and sat down till the work should be finished, and as he looked up he saw all at once how beautiful the old church was looking.

The moon outside was streaming in so brightly that you hardly missed the sun. Roger could see all of the way up to the

carved beams of the roof, and trace the figures on the great arched windows.

To study the roof better, Roger thought he would lie flat on the cushion awhile, and look straight up. So he arranged himself comfortably, and somehow – it will happen even when we are full of enjoyment and pleasure – his eyes shut. And the first thing he knew he was rubbing them open again, only a minute afterwards, as it seemed. But Grandfather was gone. There was the stove closed for the night, and the great door was shut.

Roger jumped up in a fright. He ran to the door and shook it hard. No – it was locked, and he was shut in for the night.

He understood it all in a moment.
The tall pew had hidden him from sight.
Grandfather had thought him gone home.
His mother would think that he was safe at
the other cottage – no one would
miss him, and he would not be
let out before morning.
Roger was only six years
old, so no wonder that at
first he felt frightened.
But he was a brave lad,
and that idea soon left
him. He began to think
that he was not badly off,
after all, the church was warm, the pew
cushion as soft as his bed. No one could
get in to harm him. In fact, after the first
moment, there was something so exciting
and adventurous in the idea of spending the

night in such a place, that he was almost glad the accident had happened. So Roger went back to the pew, and tried to go to sleep again.

Roger had heard the clock strike eleven a long time since. He was lying with eyes half shut, gazing at the red fire grate, and feeling at last a little drowsy, when all at once a strange rush seemed to come to him in the air, like a cool clear wind blowing through the church.

Just at this moment the church clock began to strike twelve. Roger listened to the deep notes – seven – eight – nine – ten – eleven – twelve. It was Christmas Day.

As the last echo died away, a new sound took its place. From far off came the babble of tiny voices drawing nearer. Then the church bells began to ring all together, a chime, a Christmas chime, only the sounds were as if baby hands had laid hold on the ropes. Almost before he knew it Roger was climbing the dark belfry stairs as fast as his feet could carry him.

Higher, higher – at last he gained the belfry. There hung the four great bells, but nobody was pulling at their heavy ropes. On each iron tongue was perched a fairy, on the ropes clustered others, all swaying to and fro. They floated in and out of the tower, they mounted the great bells and sat atop in swarms, they chased and pushed each other, playing all sorts of pranks.

How long the sight lasted Roger could not tell, but all at once there came a strain of music in the air, solemn and sweeter than ever mortal heard before. In a moment the fairies left their sports, flew from the tower in one sparkling drift, and were gone, leaving Roger alone.

And then he felt afraid, which he had not been as long as the fairies were there, and down he ran in a fright and entered the church again.

The red glow of the fire was good to feel, for he was shivering with cold and excitement. But hardly had he regained his old seat, when a great marvel came to pass.

The wide window over the altar swung open, and a train of angels slowly floated through – Christmas angels, with faces of calm, glorious beauty, and robes as white as snow. Over the altar they hovered, and a wonderful song rose and filled the church. The words were few, but again and again and again they came, "Glory to God in the highest, and on Earth peace, good will towards men."

Then the white-robed choir parted and floated like soft summer clouds to and fro in the church, pausing here and there as in blessing. They touched the leaves of the Christmas greenery as they passed, they hung over the organ and brushed the keys with their wings, a long time they clustered above the benches, as if to leave a fragrance in the air, and, then noiseless as a cloud, they floated to the window. For one moment their figures could be seen against the sky, then the song died away – they were gone, and Roger saw them no more.

You can guess Grandfather's surprise when his grandson ran to meet him with his story when he opened the church. He took the boy home to the cottage, and Granny speedily prepared a breakfast for her darling after his adventure. But Roger would go on telling of angels and fairies till both grandparents began to think him bewitched.

Perhaps he was, for to this day he persists in the story. And though the villagers that morning exclaimed that at no time had their old church looked so beautiful before, and though the organ sent forth a rarer, sweeter music than fingers had ever drawn from it, still nobody believed a word of it. "Roger had dreamed it all," they said.